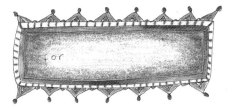

for

friends

by
Lauren White

good friends keep in special

secrets

time

advice

hope

loyalty

s u p p l i e s   j u s t   f o r   y o u . . . .

· when the world looks gloomy ·

· a friend brings light! ·

friendship is sharing

troubles

goals

treats

good fortune

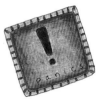

panics

happiness

good food

feelings

good friends know when to wear kid gloves...

first

♥

friends

♥

have

♥

a

♥

special

♥

place

. in troubled waters .

· a friend is a lifebuoy! ·

I like white chocolate..............

I like weak tea...............

I like hot weather............

I like oranges............

I like the town............

you like dark chocolate.........

you like strong coffee..........

you like cold weather.........

you like apples.............

you like the countryside.......

friendship

is like

a delicate flower

it needs love

and encouragement

to be at its best

T R E A S U R E D

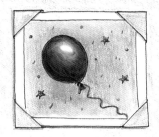

your 9th birthday

apple picking

building our snowman

volleyball on the beach

M E M O R I E S

moving in day

celebration!

the great camping expedition...

lazy days on the beach

special

friends

are

worth

the

effort

what's mine is yours...what's mine is yours...what's mine is yours...what's yours is mine...what's mine is yours...what's yours is mine what's mine is yours...what's mine is yours...what's mine is yours...what's mine is yours...what's yours is mine...what's mine is yours...what's mine is yours...what's yours is mine...

people often hide their beauty...

...good friends can always see it!

· under the stormclouds ·

· a friend is a ray of sunshine! ·

true friends see

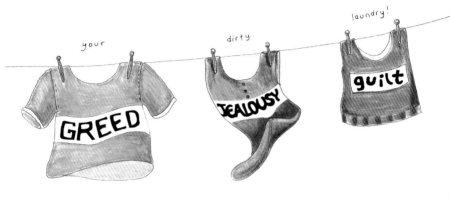

friendship

is like a

big velvet cushion

it makes an uncomfortable place much nicer!

.....friends have different points of view.....

....but.....it's never black or white.....

it's always in between!

· when life gets you down ·

· a friend is a pick-me-up ! ·

friends can

argue — make-up

argue — make-up

argue

make-up

make-up

argue

make-u

argue

make-up

argue

make-up

argue

make-up

celebrations

parties

work

coffee

weddings

holidays

GETTING TOGETHER...

sports

cinema

tea

shopping

walking

at home

christmas

lazing around

IS GOOD FOR THE SOUL

it keeps us warm
and helps us
grow

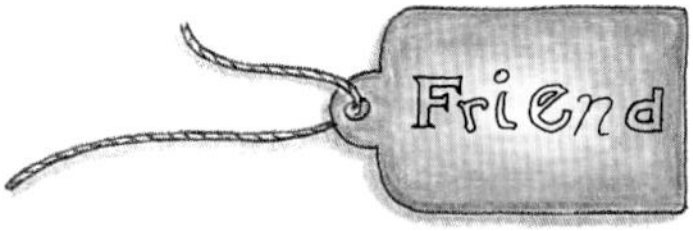
Friend

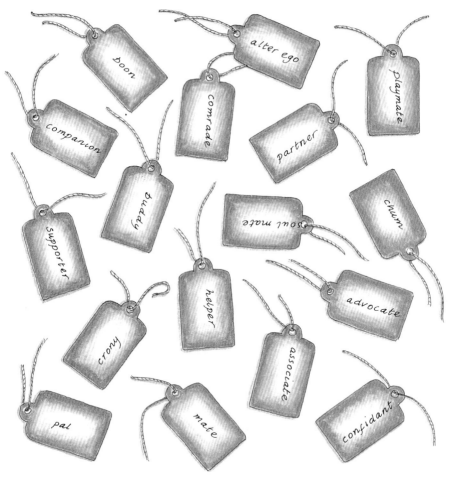

precious

friends

bring

great

riches

· when you're stuck in the mud ·

· a friend digs you out! ·

seldom seen

often thought of

friendship
is like
a candle

· when you feel all alone ·

· a friend makes all the difference ·

old
friends
are
the
salt
of
the
earth

take some every day!

· when you can't stand the heat ·

· a friend is cool! ·

friends
give
a
true
reflection

friendship

is like

an apple tree

tend it well,
and it will
bear fruit

friends give you volumes of wisdom and advice!

rough

FRIENDS

black

ups

sun

thick

WILL SEE YOU THROUGH......

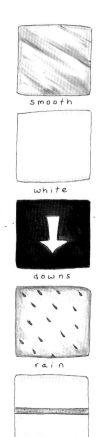

smooth

white

downs

rain

thin

ALL THE EXTREMES

friendship

is like

a favourite coat

every friendship has its:

ups

and downs.....

you can tell a good friend all your secrets ~ but they never tell !......

friendship

is like

a boat

it will carry you

across

stormy seas

when others can't see it......

...your friends know your true worth...

· when you're feeling lost ·

· a friend can show you the way ·

the terrain is often rough...

...friends help smooth the way.

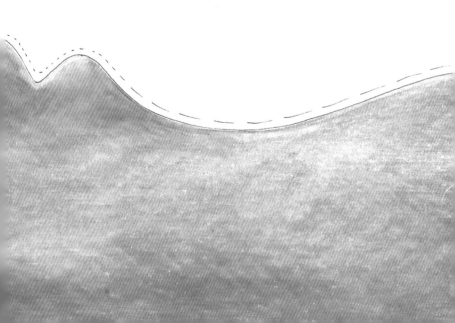

true

friends

lift

your

spirits

PROBLEM

(i) just dented the car

(ii) work — work — work

(iii) had another lovers tiff

(iv) kitchen floor is flooded

(v) 'got the 'flu

(vi) it's a bad hair day!

(vii) auntie is coming to stay

(viii) 'feeling lonely and unloved

SOLUTION

talk it over

friendship
is like
a good book

good food + good music + good friends =

a perfect evening!

far away
friends
stay
close
at
heart

friendship can be a see-saw

going out   ●   staying in

tears   ●   laughter

gossiping   ●   keeping secrets

joys   ●   troubles

chatter   ●   silence

...all for one...

...and one for all

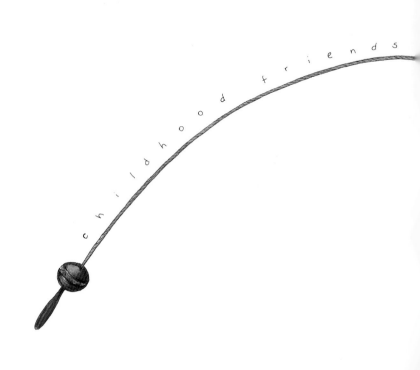

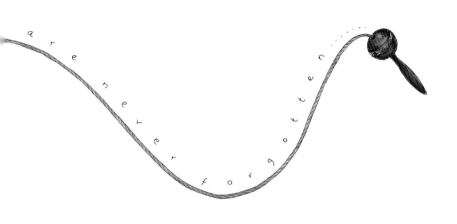

are never forgotten ....

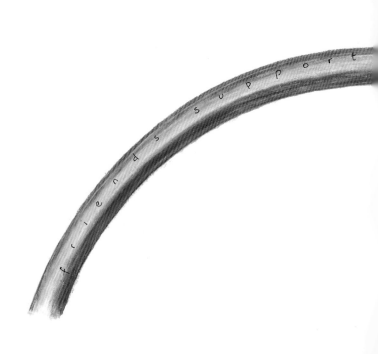

friends support

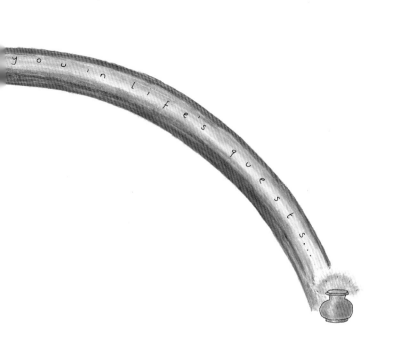

you in life's quest s...

friends cook up all kinds of plans together !....

· when you're feeling great ·

· a friend is the icing on the cake! ·

friendship connects us all

forget · me · not

"Adding a sprinkling of magic to the everyday..." is how Lauren White describes her original style of drawing. Born and brought up in the village of Cranfield in Bedfordshire County, England, she studied fine art in Hull and London before returning to Bedfordshire to work as resident illustrator for a local wildlife trust. Lauren loves playing the piano, walking her dog Jack, and she carries a sketchbook everywhere she goes. She lives with her partner, Michael, and describes herself as having an astonishing collection of marbles and a wicked sense of humor. Lauren's designs for Hotchpotch greetings cards are sold around the world, and in this book she continues to refine her distinctive style which "celebrates the simple things in life."

other titles in this series:

I Love You
Mother
Baby
Home Sweet Home
For Your Birthday

Published by MQ Publications Limited
12 The Ivories, 6–8 Northampton Street, London N1 2HY

Copyright © MQ Publications Limited 2001

Text & Illustrations © Lauren White 2001

ISBN: 1 84072 008 5

3 5 7 9 0 8 6 4 2

Printed and bound in Spain